For Mom
—C.H.

For Alice McKinley
—B.M.

Text copyright © 2019 by Christopher Healy
Jacket art and interior illustrations copyright © 2019 by Ben Mantle

All rights reserved. Published in the United States by Random House Children's Books,
a division of Penguin Random House LLC, New York.

Random House and the colophon are registered trademarks of Penguin Random House LLC.

Visit us on the Web! rhcbooks.com

Educators and librarians, for a variety of teaching tools, visit us at RHTeachersLibrarians.com

Library of Congress Cataloging-in-Publication Data is available upon request.
ISBN 978-0-525-58029-4 (trade) — ISBN 978-0-525-58030-0 (lib. bdg.) — ISBN 978-0-525-58031-7 (ebook)

Book design by Nicole de las Heras

MANUFACTURED IN CHINA
10 9 8 7 6 5 4 3 2 1
First Edition

THIS IS NOT THAT KIND OF BOOK

Written by
Christopher Healy

Illustrated by
Ben Mantle

I'm an apple!

Random House New York

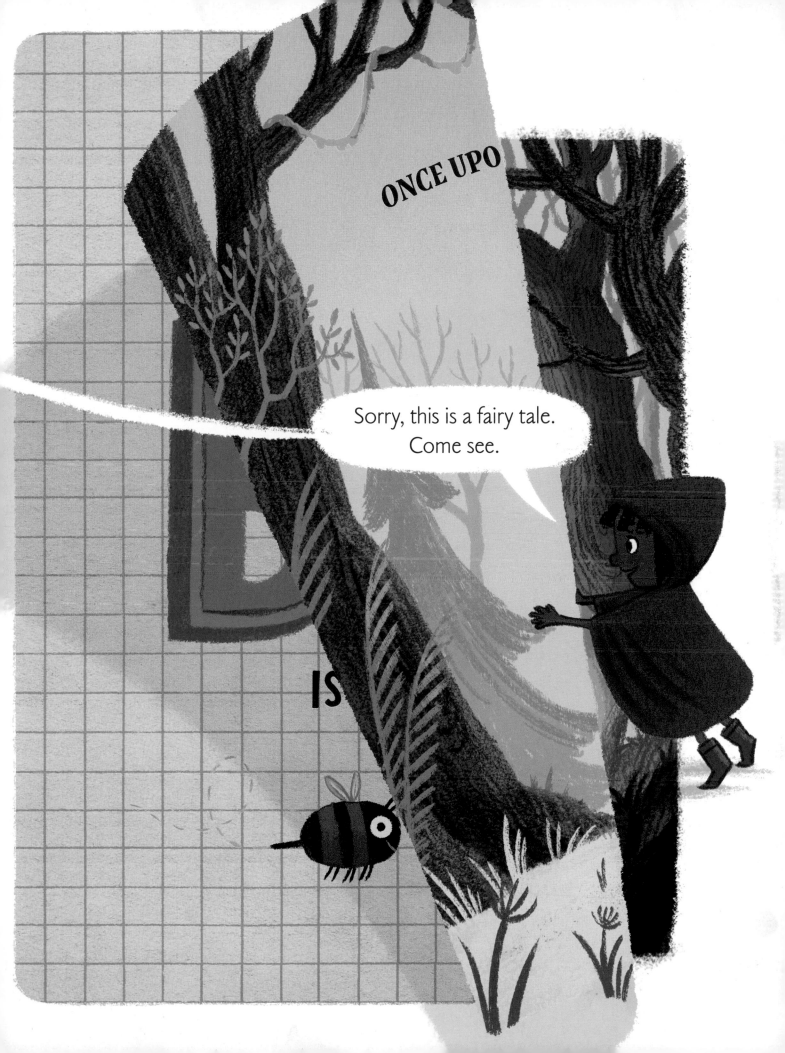

ONCE UPON A TIME . . .

a brave little girl set off into the woods
with a basket of goodies.

I'm an apple!

Hop in!

But the forest soon darkened around her. Something was lurking in the shadows!

Just then, a robot burst from the trees.

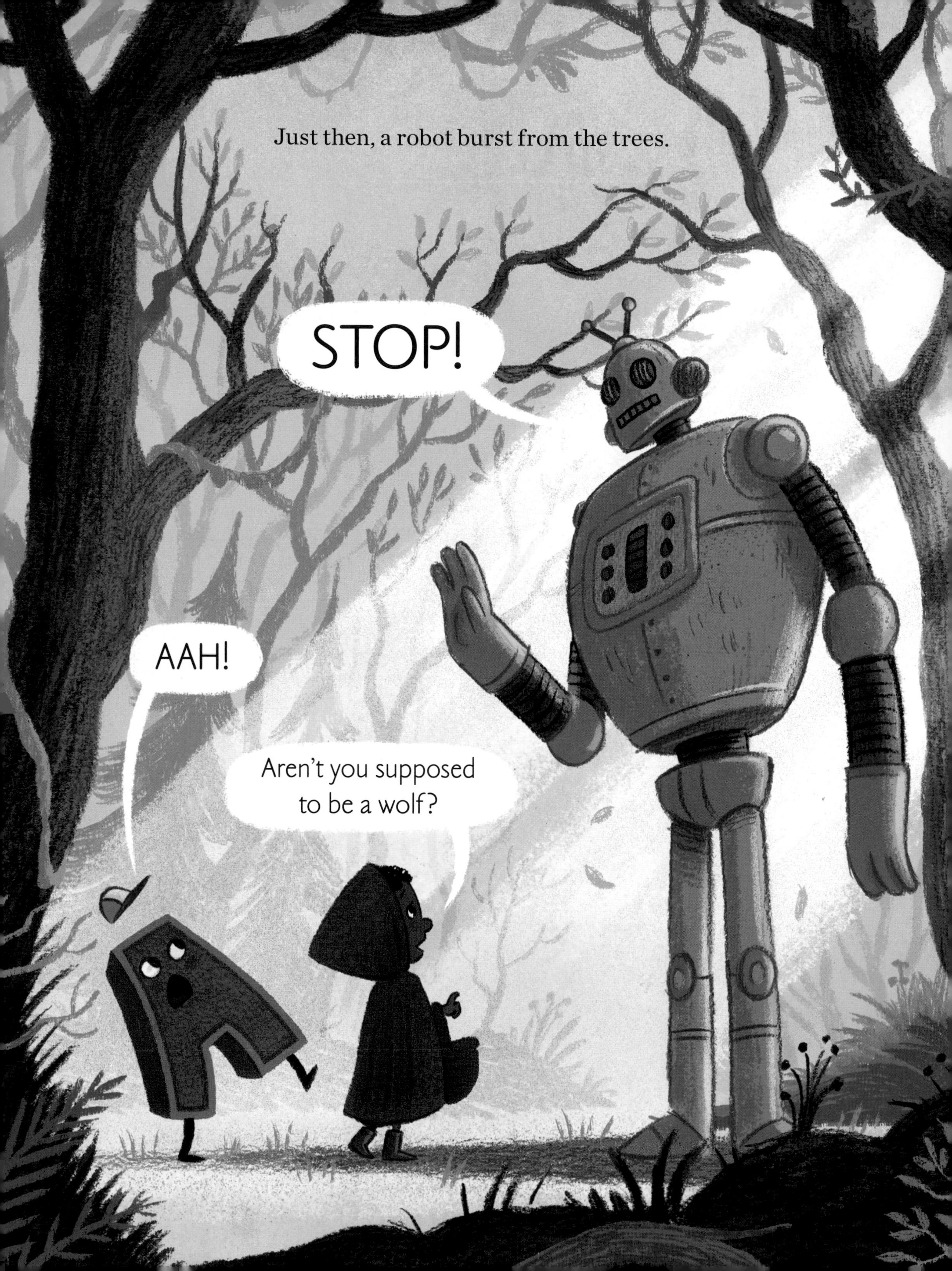

This is not
that kind of book.

The girl thought it was unusual to
find a robot in the forest, but it's not
so unusual when you're in . . .

What kind
of book is this?

Come see.

. . . the GLEEP GLORK FOREST OF MARS! Which is exactly where they were. And they were not alone! A strange creature was headed their way!

Does that say *"Mars"*? Fairy tales don't happen on Mars!

I told you this was not that kind of book!

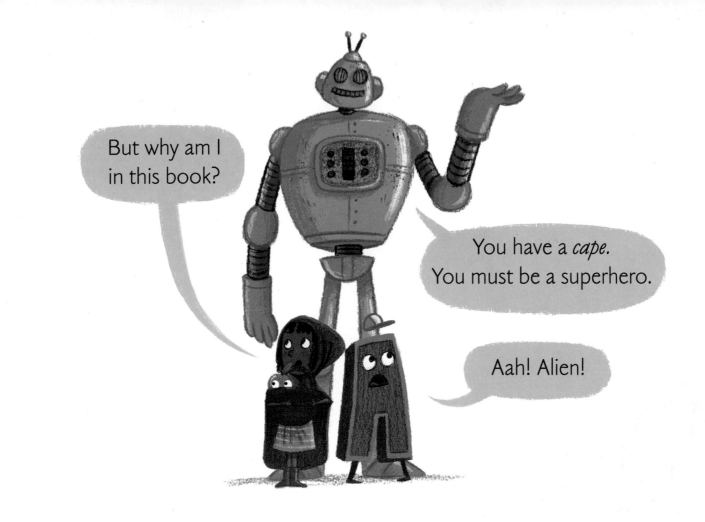

The robot, the apple, the A, and the girl who may have been a superhero ran as fast as they could.

And before the creature could reach them, they ducked inside . . .

. . . a cozy little schoolhouse.

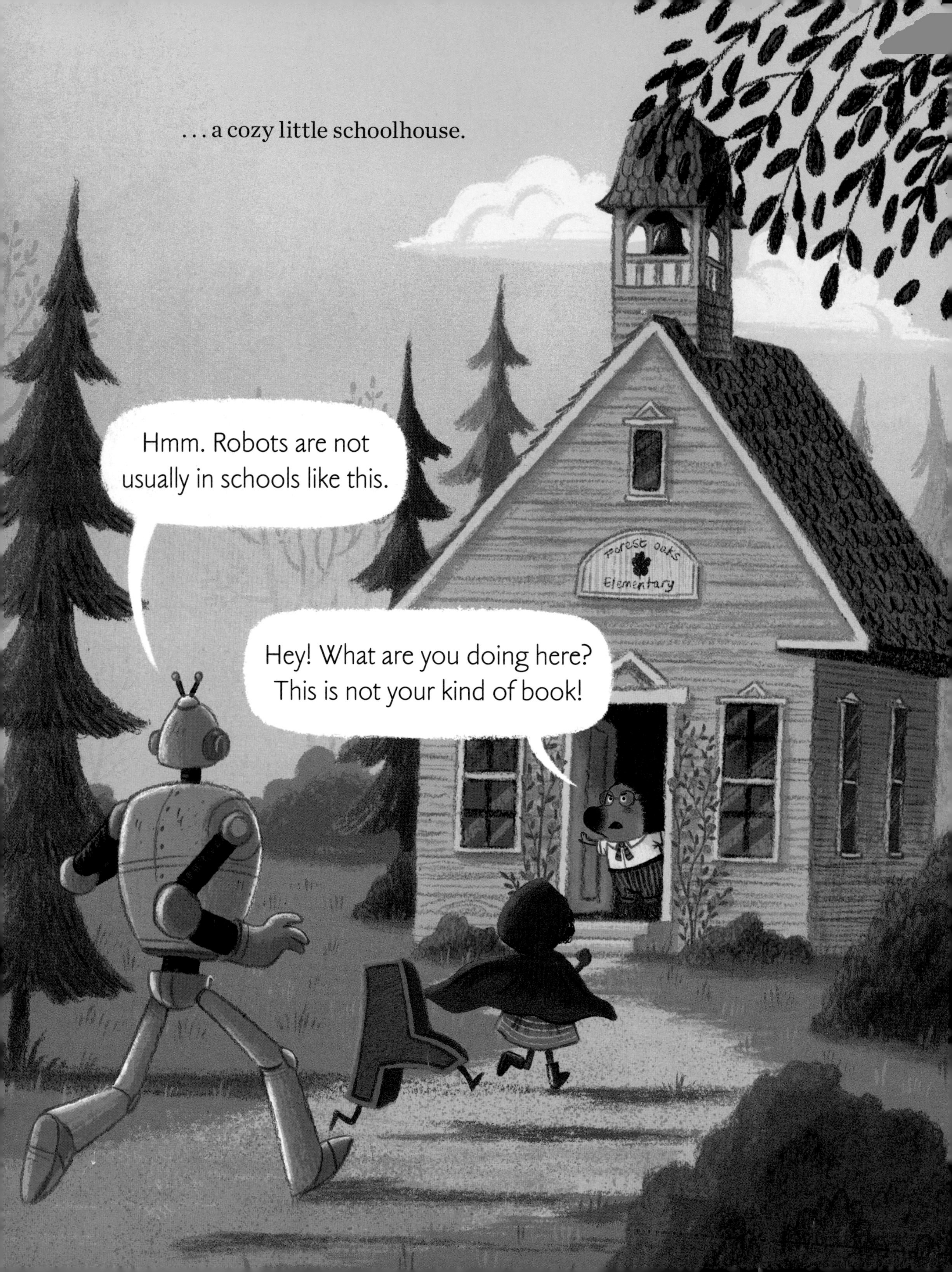

It was Hedgible T. Hedgehog's first day of kindergarten, and she couldn't wait to meet her new classmates! She was certain they would all become the closest of friends.

So . . . what kind of book is this?

The kind where all the characters are animals, but we dress in people clothes, and we go to school and learn lessons about friendship. So you don't belong here.

Ahem.

Hedgible was certain her new classmates would be other animals in people clothes. Not robots or letters or people in people clothes.

I'm an apple!

Hide on the desk. Maybe she won't notice.

KNOCK-KNOCK!

Shoo! My real friends are finally here!

I think *somebody* needs those friendship lessons right away.

But Hedgible T. Hedgehog was not the kind of hedgehog who took advice from robots or letters or people in people clothes.

The strange creature was not scary. The strange creature was just confused.

In fact, *everyone* was confused.

There are other kinds of captains. Like pirates . . .

Hey, that's my joke. . . . Knock-knock. Who's there? Pie. Pie who? Pie-rates are coming, pie-rates are coming!

Ha! That be hil-*arrrrr*-ious!

Where did *he* come from?

No, no, no, no, no, no, no! This is not that kind of book!

'Tisn't a bone-chilling tale of the stormy seas?

Do they have bananas at sea?

No one seemed to know exactly what kind of book this was. Or who belonged in it. But perhaps, if they worked together, they could solve the mystery.

Did somebody say "mystery"?

Enough! Get out! All of you! This is an animals-at-school book! There are no pirates, no bananas, no robots, no superheroes, no talking letters, and no detectives! *None* of you belong here!
I'm an apple.

Hedgible waited alone in the classroom for the arrival of her real friends. She waited a long time.

Guys?

She began to wonder if maybe she had made a mistake.

Guys?

She began to wonder if maybe this was not that kind of book.

This was NOT that kind of book.

There was only one way to find out what kind of book this was.
But it would require bravery. There would be no *backing out.*

Back? Out? That's it!
I'm going to the back cover!

Outside the book?

Thar could be danger.

The others waited.

And waited.

Finally, the explorers returned. . . .

It *was* a real kind of book. It was their book.

The mystery was solved.

And Hedgible T. Hedgehog had something very important to add.

I owe you all an apology. I never should have kicked you out of my classroom.
In fact, all of *you* are my new fr—
Hey, wait! I learned a lesson about friendship!
This *is* that kind of book! I was right!

Actually . . .

But so were the rest of you.

And they lived happily ever after.

THE END

So what if it says "THE END"? Let's have a picnic! I left a basket of goodies in the forest at the beginning of the book.

The scary Martian forest?